For Will
—M. C.

To my new friend Christy and my
steadfast friend Margery
—W. H.

Henry Holt and Company, *Publishers since 1866*
Henry Holt® is a registered trademark of Macmillan Publishing Group, LLC
120 Broadway, New York, NY 10271 • mackids.com

Library of Congress Cataloging-in-Publication Data is available.
ISBN 978-1-250-17131-3

Our books may be purchased in bulk for promotional, educational, or business use.
Please contact your local bookseller or the Macmillan Corporate and Premium Sales Department at
(800) 221-7945 ext. 5442 or by email at MacmillanSpecialMarkets@macmillan.com.

First edition, 2020
The artwork was created with 6B graphite pencil, colored pencil, chalk, pastel, pixels,
china marker, crayon, ink, watercolor (with a melted snowball), collage, transparent tape, and kneaded eraser on paper.
Printed in China by RR Donnelley Asia Printing Solutions Ltd., Dongguan City, Guangdong Province.

1 3 5 7 9 10 8 6 4 2

Snow Friends

Margery Cuyler
illustrated by Will Hillenbrand

Christy Ottaviano Books
Henry Holt and Company ✦ New York

Snow! Snow!
And more snow!

Oscar couldn't wait to go outside, but no one was awake, not even his boy, Matt.

Oscar waited
and waited . . .

until he heard Matt stirring.
Oscar grabbed his leash
and ran to his boy's room.

"WALK!" he barked.
"Not now," said his boy.
"NOW!" Oscar barked.

Matt sighed and got up, then shuffled to the back door.

"Go play in the yard," he said. "I'll take you for a walk later."

"SNOW!" barked Oscar.
"What next?"

Oscar chased
a cat up a tree,

made a
doggy angel,

and barked at
the birds.

"What else can I do?"
"I know! I'll take my own walk!"

Oscar raced down
the street.

He chased a bunny . . .

WARNING
THIN ICE
PLEASE
KEEP O

to an icy pond.

Just then, a ball came sailing through the air.

"FETCH!" a little girl yelled.

"MINE!"
"MINE!"

BACK AT HOME . . .
“Where’s Oscar?”
“He’s run away!”
“Uh-oh!”

"OSCAR!"
"Let's go find him."

BACK IN THE WOODS . . .

The two dogs dashed around trees,

up and down hills, and
across snowy fields.

"Let's build a snow
dog!" barked Oscar.

“Let’s ice-skate!” yelped Daisy.

"Let's build an igloo!" barked Oscar.
Suddenly, Oscar and Daisy smelled something familiar.

"OSCAR!"

"DAISY!"

"That's my girl!" yelped Daisy.

"That's my boy!" barked Oscar.

The two dogs ran through the snow, up the hill, and jumped on their owners.

"Oscar!" yelled Matt.

"Daisy!" yelled the girl.

KA-BOOM!
They all fell over.
And rolled and rolled downhill until . . .

they landed in a heap.

Oscar licked Matt's face.
"My boy!" he barked.

Daisy licked her girl's face.
"My girl!" she yelped.

Then off they ran.

SNOW

FRIENDS!